亲爱的爸爸妈妈们：

在阅读这本书之前，您可以让您的孩子先在左侧的横线上写下自己的名字——这可能成为他（她）完完整整读完的第一本书，也因此成为真正意义上第一本属于他（她）自己的书。

作为美国最知名的儿童启蒙阅读丛书"I Can Read!"中的一册，它专为刚开始阅读起步的孩子量身打造，具有用词简单、句子简短、适当重复，以及注重语言的韵律和节奏等特点。这些特点非常有助于孩子对语言的学习，不论是学习母语，还是学习作为第二语言的英语。

故事的主角是鼎鼎大名的贝贝熊一家，这一风靡美国近半个世纪的形象对孩子具有天然的亲和力，很多跟贝贝熊有关的故事都为孩子所津津乐道。作为双语读物，它不但能引导孩子独立捧起书本，去了解书中有趣的情节，还能做到真正从兴趣出发，让孩子领略到英语学习的乐趣。

就从贝贝熊开始，让您的孩子爱上阅读，帮助他们开启自己的双语阅读之旅吧！

图书在版编目（CIP）数据

坐火车旅行：英汉对照 / (美) 博丹(Berenstain,J.)，(美) 博丹 (Berenstain,M.) 著
;姚雁青译. -- 乌鲁木齐：新疆青少年出版社，2013.1

（贝贝熊系列丛书）

ISBN 978-7-5515-2733-0

Ⅰ.①坐… Ⅱ.①博… ②博… ③姚… Ⅲ.①英语－汉语－对照读物②儿童故事
－美国－现代 Ⅳ.①H319.4：I

中国版本图书馆CIP数据核字(2012)第273206号

版权登记：图字 29-2012-24

The Berenstain Bears: All Aboard!
copyright©2010 by the Berenstain Bears, Inc.
This edition arranged with Sterling Lord Literistic, Inc.
through Andrew Nurnberg Associates International Limited

贝贝熊系列丛书

坐火车旅行

(美) 简·博丹　麦克·博丹　绘著　Jan & Mike Berenstain　　姚雁青　译

出版人	徐 江		策 划	许国萍
责任编辑	贺艳华		美术编辑	查 璇　刘小珍
法律顾问	钟 麟 13201203567（新疆国法律师事务所）			

新疆青少年出版社
（地址：乌鲁木齐市北京北路29号　邮编：830012）

Http://www.qingshao.net　E-mail：QSbeijing@hotmail.com

印 刷	北京时尚印佳彩色印刷有限公司	经 销	全国新华书店
开 本	787mm×1092mm　1/16	印 张	2
版 次	2013年1月第1版	印 次	2013年1月第1次印刷
印 数	1-10000册	定 价	9.00元
标准书号	ISBN 978-7-5515-2733-0		

The Berenstain Bears

贝贝熊系列丛书 双语阅读

I Can Read!

ALL ABOARD!
坐火车旅行

(美) 简·博丹 麦克·博丹 绘著
Jan & Mike Berenstain

姚雁青 译

CHISO SINCE 1956 新疆青少年出版社

4

The Bear family is going on a trip.

They are visiting their aunt Tillie.

To get there, they will catch a train.

Brother and Sister look down the track.

Here comes the train!

"*WOO-HOO!*" goes the whistle.

贝贝熊一家准备出门旅行。

他们要去拜访缇丽阿姨。

阿姨家很远，需要坐火车。

小熊哥哥和小熊妹妹朝铁轨远处望去。

火车开过来了！

"呜——呜！"一路响着汽笛。

The train comes into the station.
It is pulled by a big, shiny engine.
Clouds of smoke puff out of the smokestack.
It makes a lot of noise!
Brother, Sister, and Honey Bear
cover their ears.

火车进站了。
拖着车厢的是一个大大的、闪闪发亮的火车头。
车头的烟囱呼呼地往外冒着烟。
好大的声音啊！
小熊哥哥、小熊妹妹和熊宝宝都捂住了耳朵。

Someone waves from the train.
It is Grizzly Jones, the engineer.
He drives the train.

有人从车厢里向他们招手，
那是火车司机——灰熊琼斯先生。
他负责驾驶这列火车。

Mr. Mack is the conductor.

He makes sure the train leaves on time.

"All aboard!" he calls.

马克先生是列车长。

他负责指挥火车准点出发。

只听他喊道："各位乘客，请上车！"

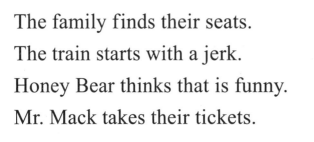

The family finds their seats.
The train starts with a jerk.
Honey Bear thinks that is funny.
Mr. Mack takes their tickets.

贝贝熊一家找到了他们的座位。
火车猛地一晃，开动了。
熊宝宝觉得这很好玩。
马克先生过来给大家检了票。

At first they go slow.
Then they go faster.
They pass their tree house.

开始，火车开得很慢，
然后开始加速。
贝贝熊一家经过了他们住的树屋。

They pass Farmer Ben's Farm.
Farmer Ben waves from his tractor.

他们经过了农场主本先生的农场。
农场主本先生从拖拉机上向他们招手。

They pass the Bear Country School.

Handy bear Gus is fixing the roof.

They go through Grizzlyville.

They see cars and streetlights.

They see stores and traffic cops.

他们经过了熊王国学校。

巧手熊格斯正在修理学校的屋顶。

他们经过了灰熊镇。

他们看见了汽车和路灯，

还有商店和交通警。

The train crosses a bridge.

They see bears in boats fishing.

They see bears working on the railroad.

They go through a tunnel.

火车开上一座大桥。

他们看见一些熊正在船上钓鱼，

还看见一些熊正在修铁道。

他们穿过一条隧道。

The train climbs into the mountains.

They pass bears skiing and climbing.

The train goes down in a valley.

They see mountain goats and deer.

火车向上开进山区。

他们经过了正在滑雪和爬山的熊。

火车向下开进山谷。

他们看见了山里的羊和鹿。

The cubs get tired of looking out the window.
Mr. Mack asks if they want to
visit the engine.
Grizzly Jones is driving.
His helper throws coal on the fire
to make the train go.

小熊们看够了窗外的风景，
马克先生邀请他们去参观火车头。
灰熊琼斯先生正在驾驶，
他的助手不停地往火里加煤，好让火车开动。

Grizzly lets them blow the whistle.
"WOO-HOO!" goes the whistle.
"Would you like to drive the train?"
asks Grizzly Jones.
Would they ever!
The cubs take turns in the driver's seat.

灰熊先生让小熊们拉响汽笛。
汽笛响了："呜——呜!"
灰熊琼斯先生问："你们想开火车吗?"
不想才怪呢!
小熊兄妹挨个在司机的座位上坐了会儿。

A freight train comes along.

At the end there is a red caboose.

It is like a little house on wheels.

The train's conductor lives there.

He waves as they go past.

一列货车开过来了，
最后一节是红色的列车长专用车厢。
它像一间装着轮子的小房子，
这列货车的列车长就住在里面。
火车从他身边开过时，他向大家招手。

The cubs go back to their seats.
They are getting hungry.
Mama has a lunch basket.
 The Bears eat as the train rolls on.

小熊们回到座位上。
他们的肚子饿得咕咕叫了。
熊妈妈带了一篮子午餐，
大家在滚滚前行的火车上吃了起来。

Soon, the train slows down.
They pull into a station.
The train stops and gives off
a big puff of steam.

不一会儿，火车慢了下来。
他们驶进了一个车站。
火车停下来，喷出好大一股蒸汽。

"Whoosh!"

Good-bye, Mr. Mack and Grizzly Jones.
The cubs enjoyed their ride on the train.

"呜——哧！"
再见，马克先生和灰熊琼斯先生！
小熊们的火车之旅快乐极了！

Aunt Tillie is waiting in her car.
"I want to be an engineer when
I grow up," Sister says.
"What about you, Brother?" asks Aunt Tillie.
"I want to live in a red caboose!" he says.

缇丽阿姨正在车里等大家。
小熊妹妹一本正经地宣布："我长大了要当一名火车司机！"
缇丽阿姨问小熊哥哥："小伙子，你呢？"
小熊哥哥不假思索地回答："我想住在那个红色的货车车厢里！"

"So do I," says Aunt Tillie.

缇丽阿姨笑了："真是个好主意，我也想住在那里！"